LITTLE RED RIDING HOOD

Retold by Heather Amery
Illustrated by Stephen Cartwright

Language consultant: Betty Root
Series editor: Jenny Tyler

There's a little yellow duck to find on every page.

This is Little Red Riding Hood and her mother.

They live near a big, dark forest. Her name comes from
a bright red cloak with a hood that her Granny made her.

"Please take this food to your Granny."

"She's poorly in bed," says her mother. "Go through the forest but don't talk to any strangers you meet on the way."

Little Red Riding Hood waves goodbye.

She walks into the forest with her basket. She doesn't see
the Big Black Wolf watching her from behind a tree.

Suddenly the Wolf is on the path.

"Where are you going?" he asks. "I'm taking this food to my Granny," says Red Riding Hood, feeling very scared.

The Wolf smiles a horrible smile.

"Take your Granny some flowers," he says. Red Riding Hood
is even more scared. "Yes, Mr. Wolf," she says.

Red Riding Hood stops to pick some flowers.

The Wolf smiles again showing his sharp teeth. Then he runs
away through the forest. He is very, very hungry.

The Wolf reaches Granny's cottage.

Granny is sitting up in bed. The Wolf pushes open the door
and runs in. He gobbles up Granny in one gulp.

He climbs into Granny's bed.

He puts on her night cap and glasses. He pulls up the quilt
and waits for Red Riding Hood to come.

Red Riding Hood knocks on Granny's door.

"It's me, Granny," she says. "Come in, my dear," calls the
Wolf in a squeaky voice. "I'm in my bedroom."

"Hello, Granny," says Red Riding Hood.

Then she stares. "What big eyes you've got," she says.

"All the better to see you with," squeaks the Wolf.

"What big ears you've got," says Red Riding Hood.

"All the better to hear you with," squeaks the Wolf.

Red Riding Hood drops her flowers. She is very scared indeed.

"What big teeth you've got," she says.

"All the better to eat you with." Red Riding Hood screams but the Wolf gobbles her up. Then he gets back into bed.

A woodsman hears the scream.

He runs as fast as he can to the cottage. He goes in the door and straight into Granny's bedroom.

He sees the Wolf and kills it.

Inside the Wolf are Red Riding Hood and her Granny.

They are alive and very happy to be rescued.

"Thank you for saving us," says Granny.

"The Wolf can never scare anyone again." And they all
sit down at the table to have cake and coffee.

This edition first published in 2003 by Usborne Publishing Ltd, 83-85 Saffron Hill, London EC1N 8RT, England. www.usborne.com
Copyright © 2003, 1996 Usborne Publishing Ltd.
The name Usborne and the devices ♀ 🎈 are Trade Marks of Usborne Publishing Ltd. All rights reserved. No part of this publication may be reproduced,
stored in a retrieval system, or transmitted in any form or by any means, electronic, mechanical, photocopying, recording
or otherwise, without prior permission of the publisher. UE. This edition first published in America in 2004. Printed in Belgium.

Usborne Beginners

Firefighters

Katie Daynes

Designed by Katrina Fearn and Josephine Thompson

Illustrated by Christyan Fox

SCHOLASTIC INC.

New York Toronto London Auckland Sydney
Mexico City New Delhi Hong Kong Buenos Aires

Fire Brigade technical advisor: Andy Pickard
Reading consultant: Alison Kelly, University of Surrey Roeham

Contents

Being a firefighter

Firefighters fight fires and rescue people. They help in other emergencies too.

Firefighters risk their own lives to save others.

These firefighters are tackling a huge fire.

Fire school

Firefighters go to fire school to learn how to do their job. Then they join a fire station and learn more skills.

At fire school, firefighters are taught how to use ladders.

They learn how to put out fires with foam or water.

They also learn how to treat people with injuries.

At fire stations, firefighters play sports once a day to keep fit.

Most fire station yards have a training tower.

Firefighters train by using their ladders and hoses to reach different floors of the tower.

Safe clothes

Fires burn through most things, so firefighters wear special outfits to protect themselves.

They wear thick trousers and big heavy boots.

Thick jackets stop the flames from burning the firefighter.

Smoke hood

They have a smoke hood and a helmet to protect their head.

Then they put on thick gloves so their hands don't burn.

When there's lots of smoke, firefighters put on breathing masks.

Bright stripes on their suits help them see each other in the dark.

The boots have metal soles to protect the firefighters' feet.

Firefighters leave their boots inside their trousers so they can put them on quickly.

At the station

All day and all night, firefighters have to be ready to answer an emergency call.

A team arrives for work and reports to the leader.

The firefighters check the fire engines, hoses and tools.

Their meals are cooked in the fire station kitchen.

Firefighters on night duty sleep in beds at the fire station.

In an emergency, an alarm rings and the lights come on.

The firefighters get dressed and rush to their engines.

The engines speed off with their lights flashing and sirens wailing.

Fire engines

Most fire engines carry water and ladders.

Hoses are kept rolled up in here.

Water is stored in a big tank inside the engine.

In emergencies, firefighters are allowed to drive faster than the speed limit.

The engine's siren and flashing lights tell drivers it's coming.

They pull over to let the engine speed past them.

This fire engine has a long and a short ladder on its roof.

The driver and five other firefighters travel in the front.

Bright stripes help the engine stand out in busy traffic.

Tall platforms

A platform engine is a fire engine with a platform at the end of a long metal arm.

The engine has four legs that come down to keep it steady.

The driver uses a lever to raise the platform.

The metal arm stretches up and lifts a firefighter above the fire.

This firefighter is squirting water onto a burning building below.

He is wearing a breathing mask so he doesn't breathe in too much smoke.

Some platforms can reach to the top floor of a skyscraper.

To the rescue

If there are people in a burning building, the firefighters' first job is to rescue them.

Firefighters put on breathing masks and check their air tanks.

They write down their names to say they're going into the fire.

Then they enter the building, trailing a line behind them.

Burning buildings are often very smoky.

Heat —
camera

Firefighters use heat cameras to find trapped people.

The camera senses body heat and shows where people are.

The firefighters then follow their line to find the way out.

Fighting fires

If no one needs rescuing, firefighters try to put out the fire as safely as possible.

They fight big blazes from outside the buildings.

Two engines are sent to most fires, but for huge fires extra engines are called in.

At a small fire, firefighters attach a hose to the fire engine and use water from its tank.

At a big fire, they find a fire hydrant and use water from pipes under the ground.

In the dark, firefighters put up masts with lights so they can see what they're doing.

Forest fires

Fires in forests are hard to put out because trees burn easily.

Careless people often start forest fires.

If it's dry and windy, fires spread quickly.

This fire has spread out of control. The firefighters will call for planes or helicopters to help.

Helicopters carry
huge buckets of
water to forest fires.

They hover over the
fire and drop water
onto the flames.

Water bomber planes scoop
water from big lakes or
the sea and drop it
on forest fires.

Sea and air

Fires can happen anywhere. They can be under the ground, in the air and even at sea.

These fire boats are squirting sea water at a fire on an oil tanker.

There was once a fire on a space station. An astronaut put it out with foam.

A light warns a pilot
his plane is on fire.
He calls the airport
and prepares to land.

Some firefighters
help the passengers
slide to safety while
others tackle the fire.

Airports have their own fire engines.
They can squirt foam at a fire
from a long way away.

Accidents

Firefighters help after road accidents. They have powerful tools that cut through metal.

A car has hit a tree and the driver is trapped.

Firefighters arrive with their cutting tools.

They cut off the roof and help the driver out.

A truck carrying fuel has crashed and toppled over.

Firefighters spray foam on the fuel so it doesn't catch fire.

These firefighters are learning how to break into a car to rescue people.

Natural disasters

After earthquakes or storms, firefighters can be very useful.

An earthquake has made these houses tumble to the ground. Firefighters keep the rubble wet so that fires don't break out.

In a thunderstorm, lightning can start a fire, but the rain often puts it out.

These firefighters have been sent out to help people in a flooded town.

Floods can happen very quickly, leaving people stranded.

Firefighters come to the rescue with life jackets and a boat.

Odd jobs

Firefighters do many different jobs. Lots of their jobs have nothing to do with fires.

Firefighters rescue people trapped in lifts or elevators.

They even rescue people who are trapped in railings.

Some firefighters are trained to help people stuck on ice.

This firefighter is rescuing an injured man.

He is lowering the man down a wire to safety.

Sometimes, firefighters are called in to rescue animals.

Now and then

Firefighting has changed a lot over the years, but fire is still just as dangerous.

The first team of firefighters was set up in Rome, a thousand years ago.

Hundreds of years ago, people fought fires by passing buckets of water down a line.

The first fire engines were carts carrying water pumps. They were pulled by horses.

Firefighters used to keep Dalmatian dogs to guard their horses. Now they keep them for good luck.

Modern fire engines are designed to help firefighters tackle fires as quickly as they can.

Fire glossary

Here are some of the words in this book you might not know. This page tells you what they mean.

 emergency – a dangerous situation where extra help is needed.

 training tower – a tall building where firefighters do training exercises.

 breathing mask – a mask that lets firefighters breathe air instead of smoke.

 siren – a device that makes a loud wailing sound. Fire engines have sirens.

 air tank – a container of air, connected to a firefighter's breathing mask.

 heat camera – a camera that senses heat and shows it as a picture.

 fire hydrant – a special pipe firefighters use to get water from underground.

Websites to visit

If you have a computer, you can find out more about firefighters on the Internet. On the Usborne Quicklinks Website there are links to four fun websites.

Website 1 – Visit an online gallery of firefighting vehicles.

Website 2 – Watch a firefighting slide show.

Website 3 – Play online games about how to stay safe in your home.

Website 4 – Play lots of firefighting games.

To visit these websites, go to
www.usborne-quicklinks.com
and type the keywords "beginners firefighters". Then click on the link for the website you want to visit. Before you use the Internet, look at the safety guidelines inside the back cover of this book and ask an adult to read them with you.

Index

Acknowledgements

Photographic manipulation by John Russell

Photo credits

The publishers are grateful to the following for permission to reproduce material:
© **Alvey & Towers** 10-11, © **Corbis** title (James L. Amos), 2-3 (Bill Stormont),
9 (J. Barry O'Rourke), 18 (John M. Roberts), 19 (Yves Forestier/Sygma), 20 (Najlah Feanny/Saba),
21 (George Hall), 24 (Roger Ressmeyer), 25 (Kent News & Picture/Sygma), 31 (Royalty-Free);
© **Getty Images** Cover (Wayne R. Bilenduke), 23 (Donovan Reese); © **Powerstock** 7, 16;
© www.shoutpictures.com 13, 15, 17, 29

Every effort has been made to trace and acknowledge ownership of copyright. If any rights have
been omitted, the publishers offer to rectify this in any subsequent editions following notification.

With thanks to

Rosie Kinchen, Jon Costello at Sheffield City Airport and Ty Robinson at Bethnal Green Fire Station